Double Decker
Donald

by Barrie Wade

Illustrated by Mike Byrne

FRANKLIN WATTS
LONDON•SYDNEY

First published in 2015 by
Franklin Watts
338 Euston Road
London
NW1 3BH

Franklin Watts Australia
Level 17/207 Kent Street
Sydney
NSW 2000

A CIP catalogue record for this book is available
from the British Library.

ISBN 978 1 4451 3782 7 (hbk)
ISBN 978 1 4451 3785 8 (pbk)
ISBN 978 1 4451 3784 1 (library ebook)
ISBN 978 1 4451 3783 4 (ebook)

Series Editor: Jackie Hamley
Series Advisor: Catherine Glavina
Series Designer: Peter Scoulding

Printed in China

Franklin Watts is a division of
Hachette Children's Books,
an Hachette UK company.
www.hachette.co.uk

For Morgan
and Eden

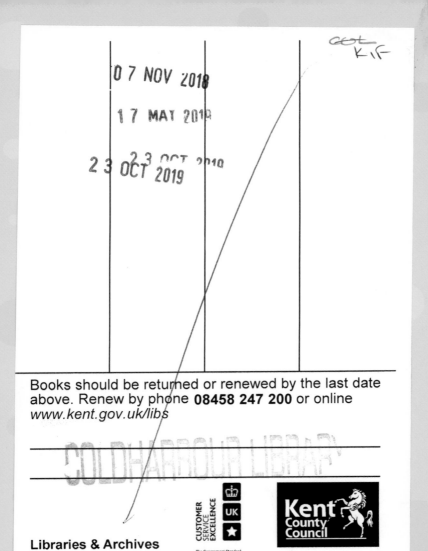

Books should be returned or renewed by the last date above. Renew by phone **08458 247 200** or online *www.kent.gov.uk/libs*

Double Decker Donald
followed the road
out of town.

He stopped at the traffic lights ...

and splashed through
the muddy ford.

He went beside the
river ...

and over the bridge.

7

He chugged up the hill.

He whizzed through the wood.

9

He spun round the
roundabout ...

He sped down
the hill ...

and over the bridge.

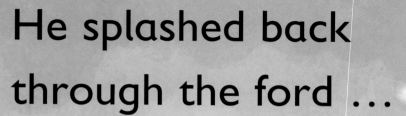

He splashed back
through the ford ...

and stopped at the
traffic lights.

He went back
into town ...

and home to his
garage ...

for a good wash!

21

Puzzle Time!

Put these pictures in the right order and tell the story!

filthy

sparkling

clean

mucky

Which words describe Donald at the start of the story? Which describe him at the end?

Turn over for answers!

Notes for adults

TADPOLES are structured to provide support for newly independent readers. The stories may also be used by adults for sharing with young children.

Starting to read alone can be daunting. **TADPOLES** help by providing visual support and repeating words and phrases. These books will both develop confidence and encourage reading and rereading for pleasure.

If you are reading this book with a child, here are a few suggestions:

1. Make reading fun! Choose a time to read when you and the child are relaxed and have time to share the story.
2. Talk about the story before you start reading. Look at the cover and the blurb. What might the story be about? Why might the child like it?
3. Encourage the child to employ a phonics first approach to tackling new words by sounding the words out.
4. Invite the child to retell the story, using the jumbled picture puzzle as a starting point. Extend vocabulary with the matching words to pictures puzzle.
5. Give praise! Remember that small mistakes need not always be corrected.

Answers

Here is the correct order:

1.d 2.f 3.c 4.a 5.e 6.b

Words to describe Donald at the start: clean, sparkling

Words to describe Donald at the end: filthy, mucky